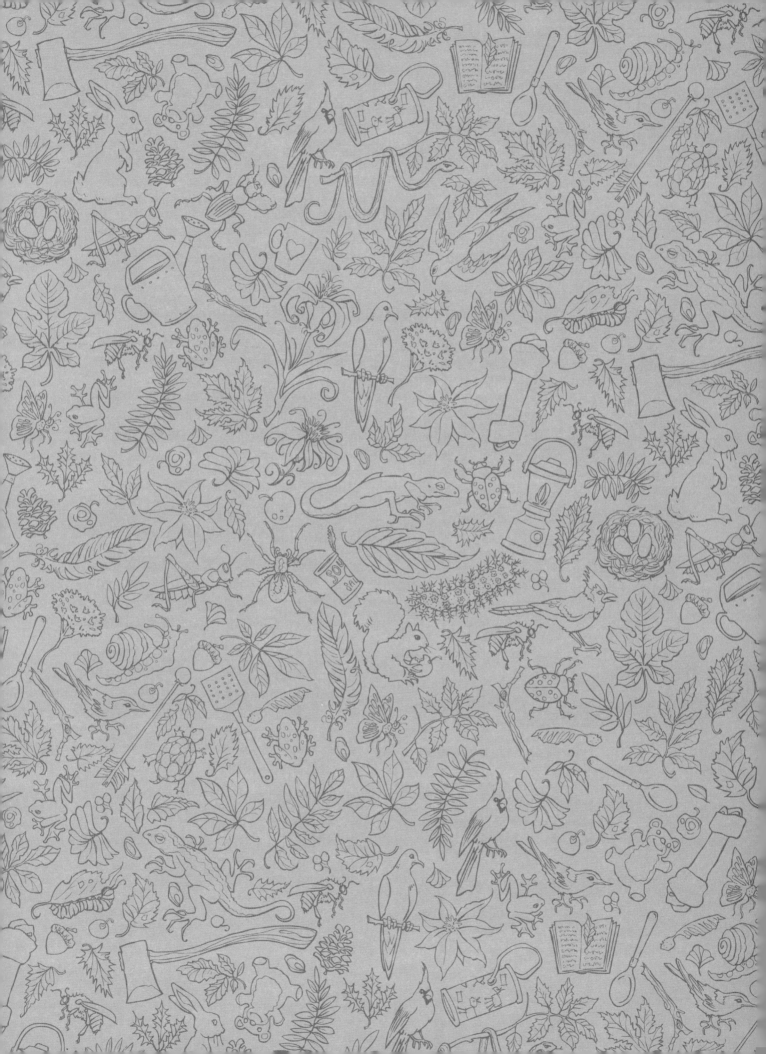

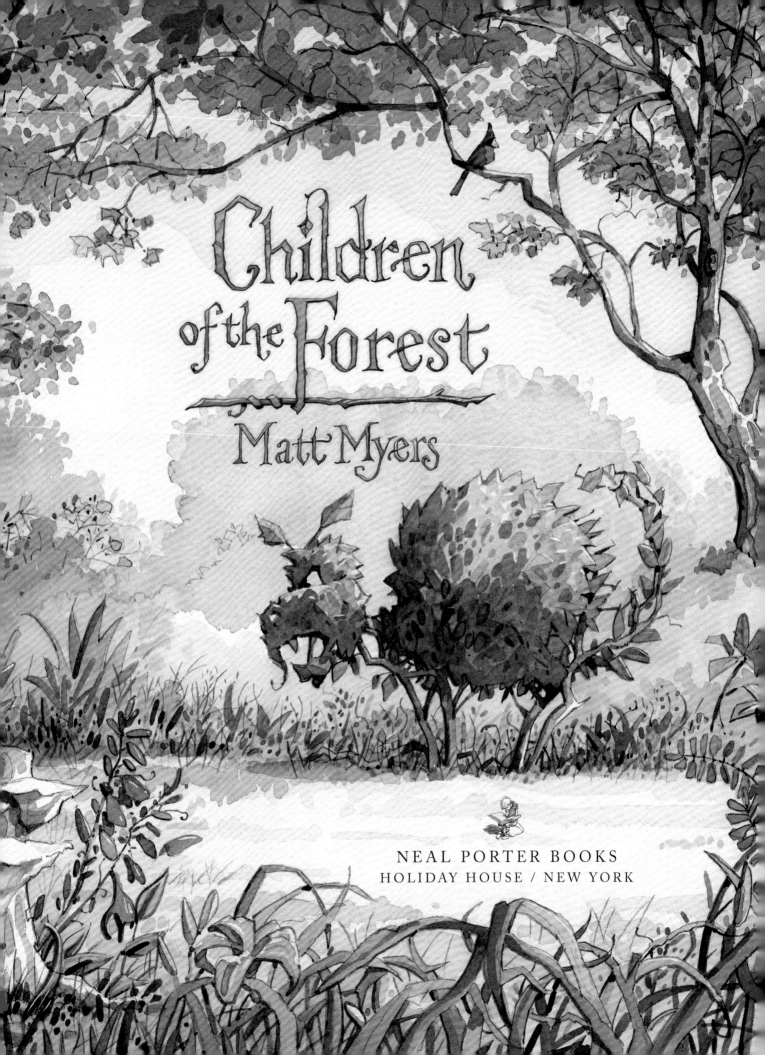

Children of the Forest

Matt Myers

NEAL PORTER BOOKS

HOLIDAY HOUSE / NEW YORK

We are wild.
We are children of the forest.

We were raised by wolves.
And raccoons. And owls.

What will become of us?
No one knows.
All we know is that Mother Nature
will take care of us.

I teach Sister
which native plants
are not to eat . . .

and how to brew tea
with ancient herbs.

We find a pioneer cabin.

We are silent, like the wind.

We take only
what we need.

A mountain lion,
known in these parts as puma,
hunts for its next meal.

I lead Sister to safety.

But she is slow.

I must abandon our food
to save her.

We teeter on the edge of starvation.
Yet Mother Nature always provides.

We follow the tracks
of a wild beast.

It is either us or him.

We will feast tonight, Sister.

The drumstick is the best part,
I tell her.

The sun is low.
We must make our camp.

I teach Sister the ways of survival.
High ground is more dry.
Red sky means no rain tonight.

Tent poles are not to eat.

No fire tonight. We have heard strange sounds, and the smoke would give us away.

Look, Sister—this will warn us
if intruders come.

We are wild.
We are—

Oh no, the alarm!

"Hello, my little campers!
I brought your water bottles.
Want some company?"

Ha! And let you take
our food while we sleep?

We send the scavenger
woman away.

"Mama!"

No, Sister! Nature is our only mother.

We are wild.

We are children of the forest.

Sister needs me.
I must protect her.

What will become of us?

Only Mother Nature knows.

*For anyone who has
needed their imagination
to take them someplace else.*

Neal Porter Books

Text and illustrations copyright © 2022 by Matt Myers
All Rights Reserved
HOLIDAY HOUSE is registered in the U.S. Patent and Trademark Office.
Printed and bound in December 2021 at C & C Offset, Shenzhen, China.
The artwork for this book was created using pencil and watercolor.
www.holidayhouse.com
First Edition
1   3   5   7   9   10   8   6   4   2

Library of Congress Cataloging-in-Publication Data

Names: Myers, Matthew, 1960- author, illustrator.
Title: Children of the forest / by Matt Myers.
Description: First edition. | New York : Holiday House, [2022] | "A Neal
Porter book." | Audience: Ages 2 to 5. | Audience: Grades K–1. |
Summary: "Two siblings attempt to live in the wilds of their backyard
before coming home to sleep comfortably in their beds"— Provided by
publisher.
Identifiers: LCCN 2021004109 | ISBN 9780823447671 (hardcover)
Subjects: CYAC: Brothers and sisters—Fiction. | Camping—Fiction. |
Imagination—Fiction.
Classification: LCC PZ7.1.M93237 Ch 2022 | DDC [E]—dc23
LC record available at https://lccn.loc.gov/2021004109

ISBN: 978-0-8234-4767-1 (hardcover)

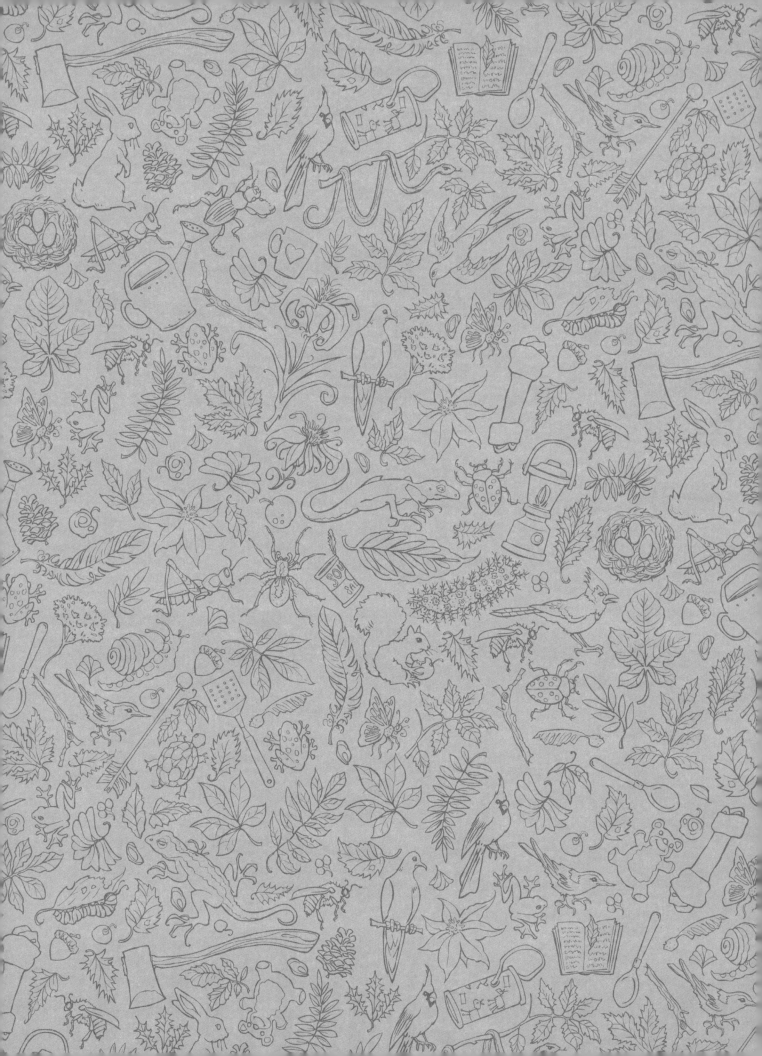